Make way for the monsters from
MONSTER MANOR

MONSTER MANOR
MANOR
Frankie Rocks the House

by **Paul Martin** and **Manu Boisteau**
Adapted by **Lisa Papademetriou**
Illustrated by **Manu Boisteau**

Hyperion Books for Children
New York

RAP *8299341*

visit us at www.abdopublishing.com

Reinforced library bound edition published in 2012 by Spotlight,
a division of ABDO Publishing Group, 8000 West 78th Street, Edina,
Minnesota 55439. Spotlight produces high-quality reinforced library
bound editions for schools and libraries. This edition reprinted
by arrangement with Disney Book Group, LLC.

Printed in the United States of America, Melrose Park, Illinois.
052011
092011

 This book contains at least 10% recycled materials.

First published under the title *Maudit Manoir, Hans,*
Le Meilleur des Monstres in France by Bayard Jeunesse.
© Bayard Editions Jeunesse, 2001 Monster Manor and the
Volo colophon are trademarks of Disney Enterprises, Inc.
Volo® is a registered trademark of Disney Enterprises, Inc.

Library of Congress Cataloging-in-Publication Data

This title was previously cataloged with the following information:

Martin, Paul, 1968-.
Frankie rocks the house / by Paul Martin and Manu Boisteau ;
adapted by Lisa Papademetriou ; illustrated by Manu Boisteau.
p.cm. -- (Monster Manor ; #2)
Summary: Frankie may be a monster, but he has a fantastic singing
voice and killer dance moves, too!
[1. Monsters --Fiction.]
I. Boisteau, Manu. II. Papademetriou, Lisa. III. Title. IV. Series.
PZ7.M3641833 Fr 2003
[FIC]--dc22
                    2006271915

ISBN 978-1-59961-883-8 (reinforced library bound edition)

All Spotlight books are reinforced library bindings
and manufactured in the United States of America.

Contents

If you're ever in Transylvaniaville, be sure to stop by Mon Staire Manor. Everyone calls it *Monster* Manor... that's because a bunch of monsters live there.

The Haunted Hills

Nerdburg

Transylvaniaville

Malibu Nightclub

MALIBU

A Scary-looking Tree

The Slippen Falls

There are lots of fun things to do at the Manor. You can stroll through the cemetery, watch the swamp glow under the moonlight, or make a few new friends!

The FEMUR Family

EYE-GORE & STEVE

This sweet little family may look scary, but the truth is that they have no guts at all.

They want to be skate punks, but they're really just zombies with bad attitudes.

BEATRICE
Mon Staire

Wolf Man
STU

COUNT
SNOBULA

She's haunted by a horrible
secret...and a hairdo
that's even worse.

When the moon is full,
he becomes human.
Well, *somewhat* human...

He isn't rich, but he *is*
totally stuck up. Thank
goodness he sleeps all day.

Step through the gate— let's see who's home!

The SWAMP HORROR

It ain't easy being a big green ball of toxic slime!

SALLY the Specter

Beatrice's mother is smart, sassy—and a ghost!

Professor VON SKALPEL

The most brilliant mad scientist in town. He's a real cutup.

FRANKIE

Created by Von Skalpel,
Frankie is one of a kind.
Thank goodness.

Take a look inside the Manor.
It might be old, but the monsters
think of it as "home, sweet home."

Von Skalpel's
Room

The Very Dark
Secret Room

Von
Lab

The
Femur Crypt

Eye-Gore
and
Steve's Pit

The Radioactive Swamp

**Frankie takes out
some smelly garbage.**

CHAPTER ONE
Mister Clean

Mon Staire Manor had a bad reputation. Everyone in Transylvaniaville called it Monster Manor and said it was haunted. They said that creepy creatures lived there and that scary sounds floated out of the house at night.

These rumors were totally, completely, one-hundred-percent true.

Still, the monsters who lived there weren't very scary. In fact, they were pretty shy, for monsters, and Frankie was the shyest of all.

1

That's him on page 1—the one with the big flat head and the small apron. Say hello.

See what I mean? He's too shy to respond.

Or else he's just frightened because you're talking to a book.

"Frankie! Get down to zee laboratory zis inschtant!" Professor Von Skalpel yelled in his strange accent. The professor claimed to be from New Jersey, but no one really believed him.

"Yes, sir!" Frankie called. He hurried to the front room, where the professor kept his equipment.

Frankie was the result of Professor Von Skalpel's research. The research was on chewing gum. More than anything in the world, the professor wanted to make a delicious chocolate–watermelon–peanut butter–anchovy–f lavored chewing gum. Unfortunately, he had no sense of taste. He needed someone to tell him whether his chewing gum was on the right track, but nobody wanted to come and work with him in Monster Manor. Also, nobody wanted to taste chocolate–watermelon–peanut butter–anchovy–flavored chewing gum. So Professor Von Skalpel made his own assistant out of spare body parts he dug up in the nearby cemetery that surrounded a small radioactive swamp.

As you can see, the professor should have stuck with chewing gum.

Frankie really admired the professor, even though they weren't what you would call "buddies." The truth was, the professor was a pretty grouchy genius. The one thing Frankie wished for more than anything was a real friend.

Frankie remembered the time he'd met

some hikers in Deadwood Forest, behind the Manor. He'd offered to get them some wood so they could make s'mores and sing songs around the campfire together.

"Won't that be fun?" Frankie had asked.

"Aaaaaahhhh!" screamed the hikers. Then they ran away.

Frankie never talked to hikers after that. He was very lonely.

"Hello, Professor," Frankie said as he walked into the lab. "What can I d—?"

"Taste zis." The professor shoved a large

stick of gum into Frankie's open mouth.

Frankie chewed thoughtfully for a moment. "Tastes like grape."

The professor's face turned as red as a cherry lollipop. "Rats!" he cried. "Rats! Rats! Rats!" Balling his hands into fists, he turned back to his test tubes and angrily began slamming equipment around, muttering under his breath.

Frankie could see that the professor was in a bad mood, so he tiptoed away. The professor would shout if he needed him. Or if he just felt like shouting.

Usually, Frankie liked to stay in the Manor, fixing things and tidying up. That was what he decided to do today. Frankie really enjoyed cleaning. Unfortunately, he was very bad at it. The problem was that he was very strong— much stronger than he realized.

Once, he accidentally sucked the professor's shoe into a vacuum cleaner. The professor had gotten very angry, and called him a "schtinking idiot," so today, Frankie decided to avoid the vacuum.

Instead, he took the feather duster out of the closet and began attacking grime. No dust particle was safe. He shoved aside a grandfather clock so that he could clean beneath it. But he shoved the clock so hard that it flew out the open window. The same thing happened with lamps, stereo equipment, pots and pans, bags of garbage, filing cabinets, small tables, laundry, and ottomans. Really, if the Manor had been full of humans instead of monsters, someone might have complained. But this household included a skeleton family, a vampire, and a ghost. As it was, nobody seemed to mind Frankie's housekeeping.

When Frankie was finished with the inside of the Manor, he decided he'd better have a look at the yard. But when he walked out the front door, he let out a gasp of horror. The yard was a mess, and Wolf Man Stu was trapped beneath an enormous sack of garbage!

"I can't believe I made such a mess!" Frankie cried.

"You birdbrain!" Wolf Man Stu yelled. "You destroyed my kennel! Come and get this sack of garbage off me or I'll—"

"Frankeeeeeeee!" screeched a voice. It was the professor.

"Can't now, gotta go," Frankie said quickly.

"Come back here now!" Wolf Man Stu screamed, but Frankie had already scurried back into the Manor.

"Coming, Professor!" Frankie called. He wondered what Von Skalpel wanted. Whatever it was, it had to be better than getting yelled at by Wolf Man Stu!

CHAPTER TWO
A Shocking Discovery

*F*rankie hurried to the professor's lab and was shocked to see . . .

"A microphone?" Frankie asked. "What's this for?"

"As you know," the professor replied, "my chewving gum research has been razzer *schticky* lately." The professor paused to laugh at his own joke. Then he cleared his throat. "So I have decided to go into a business vhere I can make zee *real* money—boy bands."

Frankie was confused. "But who will be in the band?" he asked.

The professor rolled his eyes. "*You* are zee band, you nitvit!" he cried.

"Me?" Frankie's face broke into a huge grin. "Really?"

"Who else?" the professor asked. "You are big and schtrong—and you have killer dance moves. You are perfect!" The professor pulled out a piece of paper. "I have written zis song for you." He turned to the mixing board, put on a pair of headphones, and began twisting knobs and pushing levers while Frankie looked at the lyrics. "Zis is going to be zee song of zee century!" the professor explained.

"Hmm," Frankie replied. He walked up to the microphone and began doing some warm-up vocals. "Me-me-me-MEEEEE," he sang.

EEEEEEK—POP! shrieked the speakers.

Behind his tiny tinted spectacles, the professor's eyes crossed.

Frankie whipped out a handkerchief and coughed into it. "Sorry!" he said. "I guess my voice is kind of rusty."

"Vhat?" the professor asked, shaking his head. "I cannot hear you viz zis ringing in my ears." They waited a moment for the professor's hearing to return. "Ach," the professor said finally, "it is probably better zis vay. Come—sing. Sing!"

So Frankie did. And this is what he sang:

The Song of the Century
Undead Love (Kickin' It, Monster-Style)

My brain has turned to mushy goo,
My insides are like wombat stew,
I've lost my mind—and my left shoe—
Because of my true love for you.

My love is UNDEAD,
When you call me "Bonehead!"
I know you think I'm vile,
But let's hang out awhile.
'Cause I'm hoping we can kick it
MONSTER-STYLE!

I know you think my breath's disgusting,
My neck bolt's rusting, teeth are crusting,
But my darling, just be trusting,
Please believe my love's gut-busting!

My love is UNDEAD,
It hides beneath the bed,
It lurks there like a reptile,
Waiting for your sweet smile.
Yeah, I'm hoping we can kick it
MONSTER-STYLE!

All Frankie needs is some hair gel,

new clothes,

and killer dance moves . . .

and I'll be rich!

12

"Perfect!" the professor shouted when the song was finished. "Zat is a vrap!"

"A rap?" Frankie repeated. He'd actually been trying to *sing*, not rap. "Oh, well," he said to himself, "I guess I *am* known to rock the microphone. . . ." Anyway, the professor seemed happy, so Frankie guessed that it really didn't matter.

The professor made Frankie record several more songs. After a while, Frankie's voice felt scratchy. "Can I go now, Professor?" Frankie asked. He was tired of singing and wanted to finish his cleaning.

"Vhat?" Von Skalpel said absently. "Oh, yes. Of course." The professor chuckled as Frankie left the laboratory, and then slipped a blank disc into his CD burner. "Just vait until zee record-induschtry types hear zis," he whispered as he rubbed his hands together greedily. "I vill be *rich*!"

Aoooouuuh

CHAPTER THREE
Dogfight!

"Frankie!" Wolf Man Stu shouted.

Frankie had just walked out of the Manor to clean up the mess he'd made in the yard. He'd forgotten all about Wolf Man Stu. The werewolf had managed to escape from beneath the sack of trash that had landed on his house . . . but he didn't look too happy about it.

Wolf Man Stu leaped in front of Frankie, blocking his path. "What are you going to do about this mess you've created?" the wolf man demanded.

Frankie stared at Wolf Man Stu, who was covered in garbage. "Would you like me to spray you with the garden hose?" Frankie asked.

"Not *me*, you dingdong!" Wolf Man Stu growled. "I'm talking about my beautiful home!" The werewolf lunged at Frankie.

Surprised, Frankie stumbled backward. "Whoa!" He tripped over a tree root, and went sprawling . . . on top of Wolf Man Stu, who let out a loud howl.

The cries were enough to bring Eye-Gore and Steve, the zombies, out of their pit. They were shocked by what they saw.

"I can't believe it," Eye-Gore said. "Frankie and Stu are fighting!"

Eye-Gore and Steve stared at each other. "Cool!" they said together.

"I've got five bucks on Frankie." Eye-Gore reached in his pocket.

"You're on," Steve replied, pulling five singles from his wallet. "I've got five on the werewolf. Frankie is bigger, but he's way too slow."

"I've got ten buckth on the dog!" lisped Bonehead Femur. The little skeleton had just run up behind them.

"Get outta here, Bonehead!" Steve said. "This fight is rated PG-thirteen."

Ten bucketh thayth Frankie ith dog meat!

Who let the dogs out?

It's hot dog versus Frankie— who'll be lunch?

Finally— *Smackdown* for people who don't get cable!

Bonehead hung his head and skulked away.

Frankie threw blow after heavy blow, but Stu dodged every punch. Finally, Frankie got tired, and sat down, exhausted. Seeing his chance, Wolf Man Stu leaped at Frankie and bit him on the leg.

"I'll take that," Steve said as he snatched the money from his brother's hand.

"Not so fast," Eye-Gore shot back. "Your werewolf looks like he's got a hairball."

Sure enough, Wolf Man Stu was looking a bit green around the whiskers. *"Blegh!"* he spat. *"Blegh, blegh, blegh!"* Stu wiped his mouth on his forearm in an effort to get the horrible taste out of his mouth. "That is the *worst* monster I've ever tasted!"

"Harsh," Eye-Gore said.

Steve nodded. They both knew that the werewolf had bitten a *lot* of monsters.

Suddenly, Wolf Man Stu made a gagging sound and ran off toward the bathroom.

"Wow," Eye-Gore said. "This is really horrible."

"Tell me about it," Steve agreed. "I just lost five bucks!"

Frankie rubbed his leg where the werewolf had bitten it. It didn't really hurt—it was just a flesh wound. He picked up the leg, thinking that perhaps Von Skalpel could sew him up. But when Frankie hopped to the laboratory, he saw that the professor was gone. Frankie sighed. He guessed he'd just have to sew himself up. Too bad he didn't have any more monster glue. . . .

Professor Von Skalpel was sitting in Rick Slick's waiting room, uh . . . waiting. Rick Slick liked to keep people waiting. It helped his image.

Rick Slick was the founder and brains behind such world-famous boy bands as DisGuyz, Chick 'N' Phat, and the Electric Pizza Squad. If he likes Frankie's CD, the professor thought, I vill have it made!

And Frankie vill, too, of course, he added quickly.

He glanced over the list of songs Frankie had recorded for the demo: "Monster 4 U," "Rock Me Like a Mineral," "You're Too Hot to Be So Cold," "Hi, Hi, Hi!," "Oops! I Dropped It Again!," and, of course, "Undead Love." The professor was confident that the songs were just what Rick Slick was looking for.

Frankie, on the other hand . . .

The professor pulled a glossy photo of Frankie from his briefcase, and frowned at it. Von Skalpel had hoped that he could convince Mr. Slick that Frankie had something of a "bad boy" image—that his stitched-together looks would make him unique in a field of pretty faces. But as the professor flipped through the stack of teen magazines laid out on the coffee table before him, he began to

Hello, security?

wonder. Each teen idol was better looking than the next. Suddenly, the professor made a decision. He put the photo of Frankie back in his briefcase.

"Von Scalp?" The receptionist looked around, then repeated, "Is there a Professor Von Scalp here?"

"I believe you mean Von Skal*pel*," the professor corrected her. "Zat is me."

The receptionist eyed the professor's bald head. "Hm," she said, as though she didn't believe him. "Mr. Slick will see you now." She motioned toward a large man standing at the

entrance to Mr. Slick's office. "Bruno will show you in."

Rick Slick was shouting into the telephone as Bruno carried the professor into the office and deposited him onto the carpet.

The professor turned toward Rick Slick's desk, but the record producer was facing away from him. "I don't care if the Beastly Boys are allergic to fake cheese!" Slick hollered. "They'll do the commercial for Cheezy Gobs, and they'll like it!" He slammed down the phone and turned to the professor. "What do you want?"

The professor's knees began to shake. He was completely overwhelmed. For one thing, Von Skalpel didn't like yelling—unless he was the one doing it. For another thing, Rick Slick was wearing the ugliest shirt the professor had ever seen. It was making him feel rather nauseated. "Er—excuse me, sir, but I have brought a CD—"

"Blah, blah, blah," Rick Slick cut him off. "Just hand it over."

Rick Slick popped the CD into what appeared to be a gold-plated stereo and pressed PLAY. Professor Von Skalpel glanced around at all of the framed gold and platinum CDs that hung on the walls and wondered whether Mr. Slick ever played his gold CDs on his gold stereo. The song blared out of the gold speakers:

You know what I'm dyin' 4,
I'm cryin' 4, I'm sighin' 4,
I'm liverwurst on ryin' 4:
It's your love, baby!

Mr. Slick's mouth dropped open.

I'm a monster 4 U baby!
No, I don't mean maybe,
My love's so big it's scary,
Ugly, mean, and hairy.
2 Strange
2 Be True—
Monster 4 U!

When the song ended, Rick Slick hit the

PAUSE button and sat quiet for a moment. Then he shook his head. "That is the worst song I've ever heard," he said. "It's ridiculous! It makes no sense!"

The professor cleared his throat. "Er—well, zere are ozer songs—"

"I *love* it!" Rick Slick shouted. "It's got a beat the kids can really dance to. Who's the singer?" Mr. Slick leaned forward and peered over his sunglasses at the professor. "It isn't—

uh—*you* . . ." he asked, nervously eyeing the professor's bald spot, "is it?"

"No, no," the professor said. "I am zee manager. Zee singer is Frankie."

"Where did you dig him up?" Rick Slick asked.

"Oh, just outside of zee radioactive swamp," Von Skalpel replied.

Mr. Slick stared at him a moment, and the professor gulped, realizing what he had just said. But the record producer let out a big laugh, and said, "Good one! Ha-ha! Radioactive swamp. I'll have to remember that. So—when can I meet this Frankie?"

"Oh, I do not know if zat vill be possible. Frankie is very busy. . . ."

Rick Slick was not listening. He was leaning back in his chair grinning. "This kid is gonna be a star!" With that, Mr. Slick opened his desk drawer and pulled out a large envelope, which he handed to the professor. "Here's a small advance against sales for our first record. A pleasure doing business with you, Professor Von Scalp."

The professor's eyes bulged as he opened the envelope and saw that it was stuffed with a stack of one-thousand-dollar bills. He was so happy, he didn't even bother correcting Rick Slick's pronunciation of his name.

As far as he was concerned, Mr. Slick could call him anything he wanted.

CHAPTER FOUR
Zoned Out

"*E*gad!" Count Snobula said as he checked his watch. "I've got to get to the living room soon, or one of those poorly brought-up monsters will take my seat!" Quickly, he put down the beaker of blood he'd been drinking and hurried into the hall. It was ten minutes to seven, almost time for his favorite game show, *Danger Zone*. Contestants who guessed wrong answers on *Danger Zone* were thrown into a snake pit. It was very exciting!

But when the count stepped into the living room, he saw that the Swamp Horror was already sitting in his favorite spot on the couch. Normally, the count would have asked whoever was in his place to get up. But it was no use with Horror. Who wanted to sit in a damp seat that smelled like sludge?

Count Snobula let out a sigh and hauled a chair closer to the television.

"Hi there, Count," the Swamp Horror said. "Where is everybody?"

"I've been sitting here for ten minutes," drawled a voice right beside the Swamp Horror's ear. The Swamp Horror let out a little scream.

"Relax, honey, it's only me," said the voice. In a flash, Sally Mon Staire—the only ghost in the manor—appeared. She leaned back against the couch and grinned.

"Mother, how many times have I told you not to sneak up on people when you're invisible?" Beatrice Mon Staire asked as she strode into the room.

Sally rolled her eyes. "Ten thousand?" she guessed. "But don't worry, sweetie. I know how much you enjoy telling me, so I won't try to stop you."

"Hath the thow thtarted yet?" Bonehead Femur asked. The little skeleton galloped into the room, followed by his mother, Tibia, his father, Fibula, and his little sister, Kneecap. Wolf Man Stu skulked in after them. Eye-Gore and Steve were right behind him.

"Hurry, everyone!" Count Snobula cried. "It's starting!"

The *Danger Zone* theme music chirped as everyone found seats. But the minute the words *Danger Zone* appeared on the screen in flaming letters, the screen went black.

"Wh-what happened?" the Swamp Horror asked.

"Ladies and gentlemen!" cried a voice from the far end of the room. "May I have your attention!" Everyone turned to see Professor Von Skalpel standing in the doorway, the TV remote in his hand. Frankie was right behind him.

"Turn the show back on, you miserable little bedbug!" Count Snobula cried. "And by the way— where have you been?"

No one at the Manor had seen Professor Von Skalpel or Frankie in days. First, there was the professor's mysterious trip to Transylvaniaville, which he had refused to discuss with anyone. Once he returned, he had locked himself in his laboratory with

Frankie for nearly a week. No one knew what they were up to, but everyone was certain that it was probably something gross, like the rest of the professor's experiments.

"I have been busy vorking on a game," the professor said. "It is called Monschter Zone. I thought vee could play it tonight, inschtead of vatching *Danger Zone.*" Von Skalpel snapped his fingers, and Frankie began to set up four tables with buzzers.

"Where's the snake pit?" Eye-Gore complained. "This is lame."

"Who vants to play?" Professor Von Skalpel asked. "Count?"

Count Snobula rose and gave a low bow. "I humbly accept," he replied. "As you know, I was educated in the finest universities in Europe—"

"Yes, yes, Count," Sally cut him off, "believe me—you've told us."

"I'll play, too," the Swamp Horror said.

"Me, too! Me, too!" Bonehead jumped up and down eagerly.

Wolf Man Stu stood up and was about to volunteer when Professor Von Skalpel turned to Frankie. "You take the last place, Frankie," he said. Frankie silently took his place next to the other contestants.

Wolf Man Stu growled and skulked back to his seat. "I get no respect around here," he grumbled.

The professor handed the black book to Beatrice. "Beatrice, you can be in charge of *The Mumbo-Jumbo Book of Questions* by I. M. Demented."

Beatrice flipped open the book, which quickly snapped itself closed again. "Excuse *you*," a voice from the book said harshly. "That was rude."

"Oh! I'm sorry," Beatrice said quickly. "I didn't realize—"

"Yeah, right," the book replied sarcastically. "Like I've never heard that one before. Listen, lady, you aren't the first person to try to get a look at what I've got between these covers."

"Excuse me," the professor said politely. "But do you sink vee could schtart zee game?"

The book sighed. "Fine. Question number one: What falls often but never gets hurt?"

The Swamp Horror hit his buzzer. "Um . . . Frankie?" he guessed, glancing quickly at the clumsy creature.

"Wrong," the book replied.

Buzz! It was Frankie's turn. "Rain falls but never gets hurt," he said.

"That is correct," the book said. "Ten points for Frankie. Next question: What comes out only at night, sometimes doesn't come out at all, and always has a pale face?"

Buzz! Count Snobula chuckled before answering. "Why, a vampire, of course."

"Incorrect," the book replied. The count looked shocked.

Frankie hit his buzzer. "The moon," he said.

"You are right!" *The Mumbo-Jumbo Book of Questions* said. "Another ten points for Frankie."

All of the monsters who were watching clapped politely. "I can't believe Frankie got that right," Steve whispered to Eye-Gore. "He's in the zone—his voice isn't even normal." It was true. Frankie was answering every question in a monotone.

"Yeah, he sounds like a zombie," Eye-Gore agreed. "Only, like, not cool."

"I protest!" the count shouted. "These are riddles, not real questions!"

"Fine," the book snapped. "You want real questions? You got 'em. Next question: What is the seventy-fifth element of the periodic table?"

Buzz! It was Frankie. "Rhenium."

The other monsters turned to stare at Professor Von Skalpel, who shrugged. "I have no idea," he admitted.

"Frankie is correct!" said *The Mumbo-Jumbo Book of Questions*.

"Oooh," said the monsters.

"Next question," the book went on. "What two bones lie directly below the patella?"

Buzzbuzzbuzzbuzzbuzz! "I know!" Bonehead shouted as he punched his buzzer over and over. "I know! I know! The radiuth and the ulna!"

"I'm sorry," the book said, "that is incorrect."

Buzz! "The tibia and the fibula," Frankie said.

"Correct!" said *The Mumbo-Jumbo Book of Questions*.

Bonehead glanced at his parents, who were frowning. "Thorry," he said sheepishly.

The rest of the game was more of the same. Frankie answered question after question. From the theory of relativity to the history of Mozambique, he got everything right. The final score was Swamp Horror, Count Snobula, and Bonehead: 0; Frankie: 5,420.

As Frankie stepped out from behind his table, the other monsters gathered around him.

"Frankie, that was amazing!" Beatrice said.

"And I always thought you were all brawn and no brains," Sally agreed.

Even Count Snobula gave a low bow. "I'm glad to see that there is another intellectual among us."

Frankie smiled faintly at the monsters gathered around him, almost as though he didn't remember who they were. Which he didn't.

Because the brain in his head *wasn't his*!

That's right—the professor was using Frankie to test a new brain—and it had worked perfectly. This was the first step in the professor's plan to make the world's most perfect teen idol.

"All right, everyvun!" Professor Von Skalpel said, putting his arm around Frankie's shoulders. "I am glad you all enjoyed zee game, but Frankie needs his beauty sleep."

With that, the professor steered Frankie out of the room, chuckling to himself. Yes, the professor planned to make Frankie's sleep very beautifying indeed. . . .

CHAPTER FIVE
Things Really Come Together

"Quick, Frankie: What's the capital of Namibia?" Beatrice asked Frankie when she passed him in the hall.

"I don't know," Frankie said, and walked away.

Beatrice smiled after him, shaking her head. "He's so humble."

Frankie never talked about Monster Zone. When the other monsters mentioned his incredible performance, Frankie seemed not to know what they were talking about. Everyone thought his modesty was cute— everyone except for Wolf Man Stu, that is, who found it annoying.

"All his brains haven't built me a new kennel," the werewolf grumbled to anyone who would listen.

But if Frankie was acting strange, Professor Von Skalpel was acting even stranger. He spent most of his time locked up in his laboratory. Occasionally, he would step outside and stare at the sky. Wolf Man Stu, who was busily sawing wood planks for his new roof, wondered what the professor was looking for. Von Skalpel was clearly expecting something. But what? A letter? The postman hadn't come in weeks—not since Stu had gobbled him up—but perhaps the professor was having something sent by carrier pigeon. The wolf man decided to keep a sharp lookout. Wolf Man Stu loved pigeons. They made great snacks.

By the end of the week, Wolf Man Stu had nearly finished his roof. He was just hammering the last plank into place when the professor ran out of the Manor.

"Eureka!" the professor shouted, and ran back inside.

The werewolf glanced at the sky, hoping to see a delicious flying snack, but all he saw were storm clouds. "I'd better get inside," he grumbled to himself. "Man, that professor sure is strange."

"Frankie, qvickly!" The professor dashed over to the human form strapped to his laboratory table. "Turn on zee clothes dryer—zee electrical schtorm is about to hit!"

Frankie hurried over to the dryer and

pressed the ON button. There were wires running from the machine to the ceiling and to the lab table. Once the dryer started, the wires sputtered and began to hum. "What are you making, Professor?" Frankie asked.

"Er—I am . . . uh . . . making a . . . friend for you," Professor Von Skalpel said. He didn't want to tell Frankie the truth about creating a handsome new creature to be the lead singer in his boy band. He'd find a way to break it to him later.

"A friend?" Frankie asked eagerly. "Ooh, I can't wait! When can we wake him?"

"Patience, dear Frankie," the professor replied. "Vee have to vait for lightning to hit zee rod I placed on zee roof. The electricity vill travel to zee clothes dryer, sending a super-charge to your new friend, Helmut."

"But you only needed static electricity to bring me to life," Frankie said.

"Hmm, yes," the professor agreed. "But I am hoping zat Helmut vill have a very . . . *electrifying* personality." He laughed loudly. There was nothing the professor liked more than a bad pun. Besides, he was in a great mood. His new creature was looking good—handsome face, athletic body. The professor was sure the creature would be an excellent dancer. And his brain was the same one that had aced the Monster Zone competition. No doubt about it—Helmut would be the perfect "front man" for the professor's boy band. Frankie could do all of the singing, and they'd all be rich!

Bang! Bang! Bang! There was a knock at the laboratory door. Before Frankie could answer it, the door flew open and Beatrice marched into the laboratory.

"Ah, Beatrice," the professor said. "I should have known it vas you by your delicate knock. . . ."

"Save it, Professor," Beatrice snapped. "I didn't come here to ask you for the rent. I just want to borrow Frankie for a few minutes."

"Borrow Frankie!" Professor Von Skalpel said. "Absolutely not! You have picked zee vorst moment ever—my experiment is almost complete." The professor lifted the sheet that covered his latest creation. "Behold my greatest triumph! In a few moments, he vill come to life. Borrowing Frankie now is absolutely, positively, one-hundred-percent—"

"Hmm," Beatrice interrupted, stroking her chin. "Perhaps I *did* come here to ask about the rent. . . ."

"—one-hundred-percent fine viz me!" the professor finished quickly. "Go ahead, take him."

"Thank you," Beatrice said. She strode out of the laboratory, Frankie right behind her.

The professor watched them go, and shrugged. He could finish the experiment himself, but he always enjoyed having an audience. Still, nothing could change the fact that, in less than an hour, the professor's brilliant boy band would be ready for action.

Things were really coming together.

CHAPTER SIX
Things Really Fall Apart

"Frankie," Beatrice said as she opened the door to her bedroom, "please try not to break anything."

Frankie nodded, then stepped past her through the door. He'd never been in her room before, and he was dazzled by all of her beautiful things. On her bed was a gorgeous black bedspread stitched with a silver spiderweb pattern. A collection of fine china rats sat atop her dresser. Above that was a beautiful portrait of Beatrice, framed in bone. Beatrice noticed Frankie looking at it.

"That was painted by Leonardo da Crazi," she told him. "Right before he went completely bananas."

In the picture, Beatrice was holding a gorgeous purple flower. Frankie noticed that there was a bunch of them in a vase on a small table by her dresser. That must be Beatrice's favorite kind of flower, he thought. But as he crossed to sniff them, he walked past a floor-length mirror framed in eyeballs.

"Ugh!" screeched the mirror. "And I thought Beatrice's hairdo was bad!"

Frightened, Frankie backed up into the table. Before he could turn around, the vase tumbled to the floor, shattering into a thousand pieces and scattering the purple flowers everywhere.

Beatrice checked her watch. "Two minutes, twenty seconds," she said to herself. "Not bad. Honestly, I thought my entire rat collection would be toast by now."

"I'm sorry," Frankie said as he quickly gathered the flowers. But the vase was broken—he had nowhere to put them. He gazed sadly down at the flowers. They were so pretty. I wonder if they smell as good as they look, Frankie thought as he brought the flowers to his nose—

"DON'T SMELL THEM!" Beatrice cried.

Frankie stared at her.

"I mean—er—those flowers are old," Beatrice said quickly. "You can just throw them away. Here." She handed him a blood-red wastebasket. "I should have known better than to leave those flowers lying around," she said softly to herself. "One sniff, and you would have gone totally wacko—just like Leonardo."

Once Frankie was finished cleaning up, Beatrice pointed to a large crack in the ceiling. "See that?" she said to Frankie.

"Do you mean the crack," Frankie asked, looking through the enormous hole in the ceiling, "or the black storm cloud that looks like a poodle?"

"Both," Beatrice said. "I need you to fix the roof before the storm hits."

Frankie looked at her blankly. "How?" he asked.

Beatrice rolled her eyes. "Get some *wood!*"

Frankie let out a little yelp and hurried from the room.

"Jeez," Beatrice said, shaking

her head. "How did that guy ever win Monster Zone?"

As he hurried down the steps of the manor, Frankie checked the purple flowers he had tucked inside his coat. He didn't think that Beatrice would mind that he'd taken them. After all, she'd told him to throw them away. He was about to take a deep sniff, when something caught his eye. It was a pile of wood—stacked in a triangle shape on top of Wolf Man Stu's kennel. Frankie went closer to investigate. Yes, this wood would do nicely. It already had nails in it, and everything. There was a hammer lying on the ground next to the wood. Perfect.

Frankie started prying off the planks of wood and tossing them into a heap.

"Hey, peabrain!" Wolf Man Stu said as he crawled out of his newly repaired kennel. "What do you think you're—"

Bonk! Frankie tossed another plank of wood toward the pile, but it landed on Stu's head.

"Oh, hi, Stu," Frankie said as he gathered up the wood and walked happily away. He couldn't wait to show Beatrice what he'd found.

Frankie hummed happily as he hammered the nails into the roof. True, it had started to rain. Also true, it was a little slippery on the roof, which was covered with sheets of metal and lightning rods that the professor had installed for his latest experiment. But Frankie was basically pleased with himself as he hammered the nails into place. He hummed one of his favorite tunes:

"Oops! I dropped it again—
Your favorite plate. I'd just glued it up,
I'm very sorry,
Oops! You think I'm a klutz,
But I'm not a putz, it's just—
I'm not co-or-din-a-ted."

"Ouch!" Frankie cried as he accidentally brought the hammer down on his thumb. He quickly stuck his thumb in his mouth and made a rather unpleasant discovery. *"Blech!* Wolf Man Stu was right—I taste disgusting!"

But as Frankie frowned at his thumb, he

noticed something strange. Although he'd stopped singing, the song was still playing. It seemed to be coming through the crack in the roof!

Frankie peeked through the hole and couldn't believe his eyes. Beatrice was practicing dance moves in front of the eyeball mirror.

"Work it, Big B!" the mirror shouted as Beatrice flailed about. "Work it!"

Frankie gasped. But not because Beatrice's dance moves made her look like an electrocuted chicken. No, he gasped because the voice on the radio was *his*!

Um . . . hello?

Frankie couldn't wait to tell the professor. Working quickly, he hammered the last plank into place. But just as he lifted his hammer for the final blow—*ZAP!* Lightning struck the hammer—and Frankie!

Meanwhile, in the laboratory, the professor frowned at the dial on his souped-up clothes dryer. The bolt of lightning he'd just seen flash outside the window should have been more than enough to send the dial to maximum. But if it hadn't hit one of the lightning rods on the roof, what *had* it hit?

Just then, Frankie burst into the lab. His hair was singed, his face smudged, and he was all wet.

"Vhat happened?" the professor asked. "Did Beatrice make you fix her showver radio?"

Frankie shook his head. "I don't think so,"

he said. "I woke up in a tree and all I could remember was that I had something important to tell you . . . but now I don't know what it was."

"Hmm," the professor replied. "Zat is schtrange. You *never* have anysing important to say. . . ."

Suddenly, one of the lights on the dryer blinked.

The machine bleeped.

Frankie burped.

"Do you know vhat zis means?" the professor cried. "Vun more blast of lightning, and Helmut vill come alive! Frankie, go schtand by zee lever and pull it vhen I give zee signal. Nozing can schtop me now! Do you hear me? Noz—"

Bang-bang-bang! There was a furious knock at the door.

"Go avay, Beatrice!" Professor Von Skalpel cried. "Frankie can fix your showver radio later!"

The banging didn't stop. In fact, it grew louder. Suddenly, there was a fierce growl, and with a great crash, the door came down. In a moment, the lab was filled with the stench of wet dog as Wolf Man Stu leaped inside.

"Didn't you hear me knocking?" he yelled at Frankie. "First you destroy my kennel— then you don't even answer the door! Don't you people understand that I'm a dangerous man-beast? What do I have to do to get a little respect around here?"

The professor gave a delicate sniff. "Use a little deodorant?" he suggested.

Wolf Man Stu growled and lunged at the professor, who screeched and ran behind the table. Stu leaped over the table, but the pro-

fessor was too quick. He dodged to the left, and then ran screaming out the door, the wolf man right behind him.

Just then, a powerful bolt of lightning hit the roof, shaking the house. The dryer began to beep, and the dial at the top read MAXIMUM ELECTRICITY! PULL LEVER NOW! NOW, YOU FOOL! NOW!!!!!!! Frankie bit his lip. "Professor?" he called. But all he could hear was the professor's faint cries as Wolf Man Stu chased him around the manor. Finally, Frankie shrugged, and pulled the lever.

CHAPTER SEVEN
Oh, No—Not the Lever!

The laboratory lights went dim as sparks flew from the dryer. The body on the operating table shook and vibrated as 300,000 volts of electricity shot through it.

"Eek!" Frankie shrieked and tried to turn the machine off, but the lever wouldn't budge. Then the lights in the laboratory—and the entire manor—went out.

"Von Skalpel!" someone screamed. Frankie was fairly certain the voice belonged to

Beatrice. She automatically yelled at the professor whenever there was a power failure.

Just then, the lights came back on, revealing the most handsome creature Frankie had ever seen. It was Helmut—the new friend the professor had made for him.

"Dude," Helmut said, "it feels so good to stretch!" He struck a pose, and his chest muscles rippled. "I slept like a—yikes!"

Helmut had just noticed Frankie, who was smiling at him. "Hello," Frankie said.

Helmut put a hand over his heart and caught his breath. "Dude, I'm sorry," Helmut apologized. "You freaked me out for a minute—I didn't realize it was Halloween."

"What?" Frankie asked.

Helmut gestured at Frankie's face. "I'm talking about the *mask*," he explained. Then he stood back, folding his arms across his chest. "Actually, I love the whole costume."

Frankie frowned. "But I'm not wearing a—"

"If it's Halloween, I think I'll go as the handsomest guy in the world," Helmut went on with a sly grin. "That should be an easy costume!" He let out a huge laugh.

Frankie rolled his eyes. He was sorry he had ever pulled that lever—so far, his new "friend" seemed like kind of a snob. He hoped the professor would come back soon. . . .

But, of course, the professor was busy running away from Wolf Man Stu.

"It was your stupid creature who destroyed my kennel in the first place!" the werewolf shouted. "And now he's ripped the roof off my new one!"

The professor darted down a long hall. "I'm sure he didn't mean to—"

The werewolf let out a long howl. "*O-o-o-o-o-o!* Now you have to insult my intelligence? You'd better start talking about how my kennel is going to get fixed!" He increased his speed and snapped at the professor's heels.

"Right—right!" the professor said quickly, panting between words. "I'll send Frankie—*pant pant*—over—*pant pant*—in zee morning—"

Wolf Man Stu put on a burst of speed. In a flash, he reached out and grabbed the professor's leg, held him upside down, and gave him a hearty shake. "What about *tonight*?" the wolf man demanded. "It's raining!"

"You could sleep in my laboratory. . . ." the professor suggested hopefully.

"In the *lab*?" Wolf Man Stu demanded. "Listen—don't you see how *ferocious* I am?" He bared his fangs at the professor, who let out a little scream. Then the werewolf plunged his hand into the professor's pocket, and drew out a key. "*You* sleep in the lab," Wolf Man Stu said. "I'm sleeping in *your* room."

"Vhy, of course," the professor agreed heartily. "Of course—no problem at all! And now if you'll excuse me—" But, of course, he couldn't go anywhere because Wolf Man Stu was still holding him upside down.

Wolf Man Stu gave Von Skalpel another shake. "What's the hurry, Professor?" he asked. "I've got all night to chat. And I am not finished with you yet. . . ."

Meanwhile, back at the lab, Helmut had discovered the professor's full-length mirror.

"Man, am I gorgeous!" he said as he struck a pose and checked out his reflection.

Frankie sighed. He looked around the lab, trying to find something he could discuss with Helmut. His eyes fell on the flowers he had taken from Beatrice's room. Frankie pulled them from the jar they were in and held them out to Helmut, who was still chatting with himself in the mirror.

"With the shades"—he flipped his sunglasses down over his eyes—"I'm cool. Without the shades"—he pushed them back on top of his head—"I'm relaxed. With the sh—"

"Excuse me," Frankie interrupted him.

"Would you like to see my flowers?"

"Not now, dude," Helmut replied. "I'm trying to figure out my *attitude*." Helmut turned back toward the mirror. "With the shades— I'm cool. Without the shades—I'm re—"

But Frankie wouldn't give up. He tapped Helmut on the shoulder to try to get his attention. Unfortunately, a tap from Frankie is much like a punch from anyone else. Helmut reeled under the force of the blow.

"Okay, okay!" Helmut yelled. "I'll see your flowers!"

And that's when Helmut leaned forward and took a big, fat sniff just as the door to the lab flew open and the professor hurried in.

"Professor!" Frankie cried, quickly stuffing the flowers back in their jar. "Where have you been?"

Von Skalpel rolled his eyes. "Let me just say zat, sanks to you, I had to cook a five-course meal for a certain verevolf!" But the professor stopped short when he saw his new creation standing before him. "Frankie!" he cried. "You pulled zee lever?"

Frankie shuffled his feet. "Um . . . sorry?"

"Sorry!" Professor Von Skalpel cried. "But zat is vonderful—he is magnificent! He is fantaschtic! He is—"

"Excuse me, lady, will you help me find my little blue monkey?" Helmut asked suddenly in a baby voice. "He talks and sings me lullabies." With that, Helmut began to skip around the laboratory. "Monkey, monkey!" he sang out in a high-pitched voice. "Where are you, little talking monkey?"

Professor Von Skalpel stared at Frankie, who shrugged. "He was pretty boring a minute ago," Frankie said. "But now he's getting interesting!" He didn't realize that Helmut had gone crazy the minute he sniffed Beatrice's flowers.

"Do you like watermelon?" Helmut asked the professor. "My little monkey likes it—have you seen him?"

"B-b-but—" the professor stammered, "vhat happened to his brain?" He frowned at Frankie. "It must have gotten ruined vhen I put it in *your* head!"

"But I never asked you about a little blue monkey!" Frankie insisted.

"Good point," the professor admitted. He sighed. "Oh, vell, I guess it is back to zee scrap heap with zis one," he said as he nudged Helmut back to the laboratory table.

"Hee-hee!" Helmut giggled. "That tickles!" He gave the professor a hug. "Will you be my mommy?"

The professor groaned. "Yes, yes," he said impatiently. "Now go to sleep for mommy. . . ."

Helmut obediently lay down on the table and closed his eyes. The professor breathed a sigh of relief. But after a moment, Helmut's eyes popped open again. "Will you sing me a song?" Helmut asked. "My little blue monkey always sings—"

"I do not know any songs," the professor snapped. "Now go to sleep!"

Helmut began to cry. Loudly. With big *boohoo*s. Frankie felt kind of sorry for him. "Professor—allow me," Frankie said. With that, he began to sing the first bars of "Undead Love" in a soft voice.

The professor smiled softly as he listened. Frankie really is very talented, he decided. It's too bad he's just so ugly. At that moment, the professor noticed the flowers on a nearby table. "Vhat pretty flowvers!" he exclaimed.

And the professor leaned over to smell them. . . .

CHAPTER EIGHT
Saved by the Bell

Just before the professor's nose reached the flowers, the doorbell rang!

The professor straightened up, and frowned. "Who could zat be?" he wondered aloud. "Zhere is a horrible schtorm outside." The doorbell rang again. *Dingdong dingdong!* Whoever it was, he clearly wasn't going away.

"Frankie, please schtrap Helmut to zee table vile I deal viz zis, vould you?" Professor Von Skalpel asked. The creature nodded, and the professor sighed and trudged up the stairs.

"Coming, coming," the professor muttered as the doorbell continued to ring. He opened the door and gaped at what he saw.

"Stanley Frye, at your service," chirped the small man. He was dressed in a blue jacket, shorts, and a jaunty cap. He gave the professor a snappy salute, grinning in spite of the pouring rain.

"Vee do not vant any," the professor said, slamming the door in Stanley's face.

The professor turned away just as the doorbell began to ring again—urgently. "Vhat?" Von Skalpel asked as he opened the door.

Stanley was still saluting. "I don't think you understand, sir. I'm your new postal delivery person, and I have some mail for a Mister . . ." Stanley stopped saluting long enough to look at his clipboard. "Frankie."

That was when the professor noticed that there was a large bag next to Stanley. In fact— there were eight large bags of mail.

"Frankeeeee!" the professor yelled.

Frankie thundered up the stairs like a herd of drunken elephants. "Yes, Professor?" he asked, stepping into the hall.

"Help me drag zees bags into zee hall." Together, the professor, Stanley, and Frankie hauled the heavy sacks into the house.

"Sanks," the professor said as he showed Stanley to the door.

"At your serv—" the mailman said as the professor slammed the door in his face. There is no point in being nice to a mailman in this house, the professor thought. Wolf Man Stu always gobbles them up before you really get to know them.

When the professor turned around, his mouth dropped open at what he saw. One of the sacks had come open, spilling letters all over the floor. Frankie was holding a card in his hand, frowning. He looked up at the professor. "What's this?" Frankie asked.

The professor cleared his throat. "Vhat is vhat?" he asked innocently.

"'Dear Frankie,'" Frankie read from the card. "'I'm your biggest fan. . . . *Ooops! I Dropped It Again* is, like, the story of my life. . . .'" Frankie pulled another letter out of the pile. "'Dear Frankie, I think you are the greatest singer in the world!'" Frankie looked at the professor, as he ripped open another letter. "'*Kjaer Frankie, Jeg elsker deres sang!*'" he read aloud.

"Ha!" the professor cried. "You do not even know vhat zee last one said."

Frankie rolled his eyes. "Please, Professor," he said angrily. "My Norwegian isn't great, but I think that I can translate a basic sentence like 'I love your song.'"

"All right, all right!" the professor shouted. "I gave your demo to Rick Slick and he put it on the radio!"

"I can't believe you didn't tell me about

this!" Frankie hollered. "I'm famous? And I didn't even know?"

"Er—vell—I vas going to tell you—" the professor hedged.

Frankie folded his arms across his chest. "I have some demands."

Professor Von Skalpel sighed. "First zee verevolf, now you—"

Frankie growled.

"Yes, yes, of course—you have demands," the professor said quickly. "Vhat are zey?" He started to sweat, thinking about the money Rick Slick had given him. He'd spent most of it buying the body parts to make Helmut.

"First," Frankie said, "I want a pen and some paper, so I can write to my fans." He gestured to the sacks of mail.

The professor nodded. "Fine," he said. "Vhat else?"

Frankie thought for a minute. "That's it," he said.

"Zat is—" The professor coughed. "Zat is *it?*"

Frankie nodded.

"Well, of course you can have zat!" the professor said. He and the creature grinned at one another, and the professor realized that Frankie really was his best creation ever. Why had he even bothered trying to make another one? Which reminded him . . .

"Now, if you'll excuse me," the professor said, "I believe I have to take out zee garbage."

After that, things calmed down around the Manor. Frankie rebuilt Wolf Man Stu's kennel, but Wolf Man Stu griped that he would have been better off fixing it himself. He said that Frankie had painted the roof the wrong shade of red. "How can I frighten people when it looks like I live in a barn?" Stu grumbled. Plus, he complained that the roof was leaky.

Von Skalpel enjoyed his new side job as Frankie's official manager. Rick Slick wanted to come to the house to meet his newest star, but Von Skalpel explained that Frankie was very shy. "He does not vant his face on any of zee album covers. He does not vant to be hounded by fans," the professor said to Mr. Slick. "And he has decided to go by zee name of Mischter-E-Us," the professor explained over the phone. "He sinks it makes him seem—uh—myschterious." It was kind of dumb, but Rick Slick bought it. And Mister-E-Us's fans loved it.

Frankie continued to help the professor with his experiments during the day, and to write to his fans and record new songs at night. Frankie didn't mind that the professor took the money from the songs. After all, what did Frankie need money for? He had everything he needed. He even got to listen to his own music on the radio while he did the housecleaning. And his latest songs, "Waterin' the Houseplant of Love" and "Cobwebs on My Heart," were huge successes.

What more could a monster ask for?